Advance Praise for **Future School:**

When you were a kid, did you ever feel that your family–your friends–your teachers–didn't understand you? Don't bother to answer–of course you did. We all did. And chances are…you (we) were right. But now, writer David Ullendorff and artist Ron Harris demonstrate, in this unique blend of scintillating prose and wildly entertaining graphic novel, that the only thing worse than those who don't understand you–may be those who do, and who want to use your special gifts for their own dire purposes. Danny Gorman and Codie Brown are the everykid heroes of a thrilling and exceptionally human story that is likely to cause you to rethink everything you ever thought you knew about the American educational system…and to enjoy yourself tremendously while doing so!

—**Roy Thomas,** *former Marvel Comics Editor-in-Chief,*
legendary writer of Conan the Barbarian,
The Avengers, Captain Marvel, *and countless*
other series.

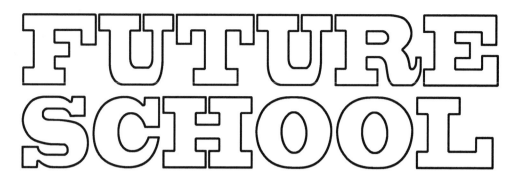

FUTURE SCHOOL

Written by **DAVID ULLENDORFF**
Drawn by **RON HARRIS**

Book Design and Production: Pageturner Graphic Novels, Pete Friedrich.
Editor: Joan Hilty

Cataloging-in-Publication Data has been applied for and may be obtained from the
Library of Congress.

ISBN 978-0-578-59804-8

Printed and bound in the United States.
10 9 8 7 6 5 4 3 2 1

Chapter 1

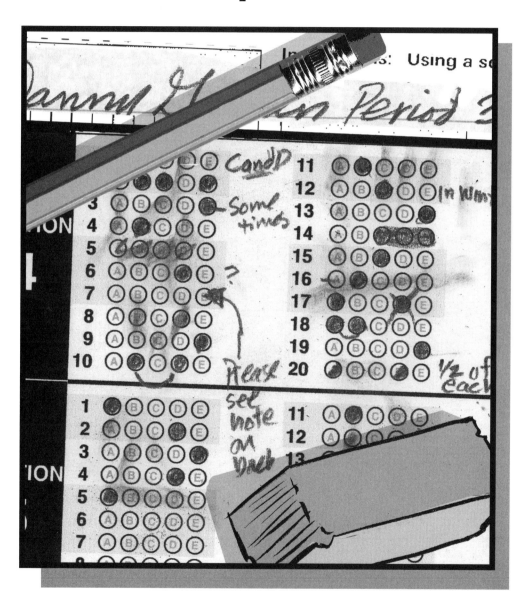

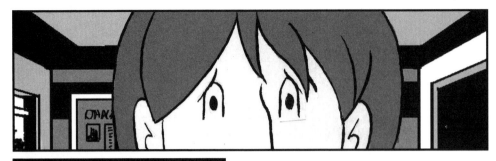

Mr. Walker projected a shockwave of dread, like an airplane breaking the sound barrier, as he moved down the row of 7th graders, returning tests. Danny watched him approach, fearing the worst.

Despite a heroic effort, he was failing school and multiple choice tests were his worst enemy. Every possible answer could be right, or wrong, if you thought about it too much. And Danny always thought about it too much.

Another D. It was time to leave his parents a note and join the French Foreign Legion, or the circus, or maybe a French circus. But before he did that he'd confront Mr. Walker after class, one last time. Surely an accredited teacher, a *professional educator,* would understand and change his grade. Maybe the two of them would even laugh about the whole thing next week, over chicken tenders in the cafeteria.

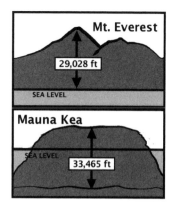

Danny followed Walker out into the hall. "Mr. Walker?" Walker kept moving, eyes fixed on the teachers' lounge straight ahead. Danny jogged behind him.

"The tallest mountain in the world is Mauna Kea, in Hawaii."

"Mount Everest," Walker replied, speeding up.

"Not if you measure it from the base, underwater."

"Get a life, Danny."

"And more tigers do live in Texas than anywhere else. As pets."

"The question said native habitat."

"It *is* native to them."

Walker disappeared into the teachers' lounge, shutting the door in Danny's face.

Danny continued talking at the door. "And that feeling, when you have to go to the bathroom–it's a sense, just like seeing and hearing." Some passing kids stopped and stared at Danny seemingly talking to himself. Danny waved feebly at them and turned away.

Danny walked home, the D weighing on him like Mauna Kea. A second D, placed on top, would give him a B. That had worked in the past. More modestly, a mirror image of the D with the vertical line blotted out was a C. That would arouse less suspicion. The gutsy move, of course, was to turn the D ninety degrees counterclockwise, add two skinny legs, and give himself an A. Just like any answer could be right or wrong, every letter could be any other letter, if you thought about it too much.

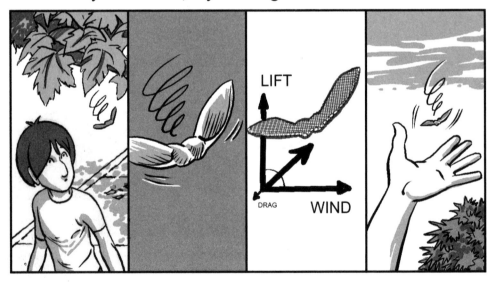

A sudden gust blew a seed pod off the maple tree in front of his house. He watched it spin elegantly to the ground, lost in the miracle of it all, experiencing the forces of gravity, wind, and friction along with the tiny object as if he and the seed pod were one and the same.

Danny was supposed to be studying for tomorrow's big geography quiz, but that could wait. The falling maple seed pod had given him an idea for a new kind of paper airplane.

He carefully traced the outline of the seed pod onto a piece of paper. The heavy nose and tiny wings made it spin like a... propeller? Could that be it?

Sofia knocked once and entered without waiting for a reply. Danny quickly dropped the scissors and picked up the geography book.

"What is that?" she asked.

"A geography book."

Sofia pointed to the maple seed pod cut-outs. *"That."*

"A country...Cuba."

"What is the capital of Burkina Faso?"

"Jumbopoop?"

"Ouagadougou. You haven't been studying."

Harvey slipped into the room. His eyes went straight to Danny's paper cut-outs.

"Maple seed pod."

Danny waved at his dad to shut up.

Sofia, fuming, pulled the textbook from Danny's hand and slammed it into Harvey's chest.

Danny picked up the seed pod from the sidewalk and examined it closely. What was its secret? Suddenly Harvey, his dad, called out to him from the garage and asked, for the trillionth time, the stupidest question ever asked by a parent in the history of the universe.

"Danny, how was school?"

"I'd tell you, but then you'd have to kill me," Danny replied.

"I think the joke is: 'I'd tell you, but then *I'd* have to kill *you*.'"

"I wasn't joking."

Harvey took a deep breath. "Another C?"

Danny flattened his hand and lowered it toward the ground. Harvey gasped.

"You got a D?"

Danny mother, Sofia, exited the front door smiling.

"Danny, how was school?"

Danny grimaced. A trillion and one.

fakebook   Home   Profile   Friends   Inbox   The Gormans   Settings   Logout

The Gorman Family

Wall   Info   Video   Pictures   >>

The Grand Vacation
63 Photos

The Master Chef at Work
12 Photos

Home Office Confidential
28 Photos

MUSIC CHAMPION
Kurt plays Mozart's *Figaro* on ordinary cookware!

DESSERT CHAMPION
See Lewis' life-size chocolate igloo!

BUG TRAINER CHAMPION
George recreates Togo's flag with 1,248 garden insects!

OBSOLETE TECH CHAMPION
Javier's 1945 vacuum cleaner doubles as a drone!

ILLUSION CHAMPION
Kim makes lifelike drawings that look like the real thing!

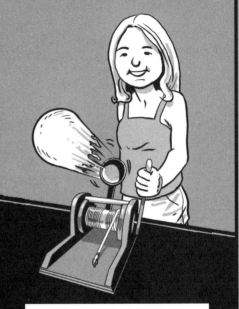

CATAPULT CHAMPION
Roxie's ice cream catapult fires French Vanilla at 65 MPH!

CAMOUFLAGE CHAMPION
Oliver is...where is Oliver, anyway?

SPITTING CHAMPION
Codie performs wonders with precision target spitting!

00-10:5...
...me Room
...0:50-11:00:
Passing Period
11:00-12:00 PM
Lunch/Recess
12:00-12:50:
...Track B Classro...

I'M DANNY GORMAN, AND I'M TRYING OUT TO BE THE ULTIMATE ALMANAC'S PAPER PLANE CHAMPION!

REC

THIS IS MY AIR GLIDER NUMBER 17, THREE MONTHS IN THE MAKING!

I DESIGNED IT TO REPLICATE THE LONG-DISTANCE SOARING OF AN ALBATROSS!

WHEN I LAUNCH THE PLANE, THESE UPPER WAVE SURFACES WILL FLAP THE MAIN WINGS LIKE A REAL BIRD! THEN THEY'LL DROP OFF AND THE GLIDER WILL SOAR!

AFTER CIRCLING THE SCHOOLYARD, IT'LL MAKE A SOFT LANDING RIGHT WHERE I'M STANDING!

I CALL IT NUMBER 17 BECAUSE I TESTED SIXTEEN SCALE MODELS FIRST! THEY ALL WORKED!

NOW IT'S TIME TO FLY THE FULL-SIZED PLANE!

Danny didn't accomplish his dream of making it into the Ultimate Almanac, but video footage of his exploits found its way onto YouTube and quickly went viral...

...spreading until the buzz came to the attention of the **Secretary of Education** in Washington, D.C.

Chapter 2

PRIME, MR. AND MS.

ROW 12, SEATS F AND G. WOULD YOU REMOVE YOUR HAT, SIR?

THE HAT? OH, YES, THE HAT.

NOT A HAT, REALLY. JUST A...

...PIECE OF STRING!

THE EDUCATION OF OUR CHILDREN IS A NATIONAL SECURITY ISSUE.

PROMISE ME, NO VENTRILOQUISM TONIGHT. THIS IS SUPPOSED TO BE A SERIOUS EVENT.

I PROMISE I WON'T THROW MY VOICE.

THANKS TO THE POLICIES OF THE PREVIOUS ADMINISTRATION, CHILDREN IN OTHER COUNTRIES ARE SMARTER THAN US.

BUT THAT'S ABOUT TO CHANGE, THANKS TO TONIGHT'S GUEST OF HONOR, *DR. ALEXANDER NING!*

SECRETARY OF EDUCATION NING HAS REVOLUTIONIZED EDUCATION BY CREATING THE SCHOOL OF THE FUTURE: *THE ACADEMY OF EXCELLENCE AND TRANSFORMATION!*

cam 1

rec
15:03:16

Sofia leaned in, knuckles on the table.

"The Ultimate Almanac?" she said, her voice steely.

Danny looked down. He couldn't meet her eyes.

"It's a website run by kids," he muttered. "Sort of like the Guinness Book of World Records. I was trying to get in as the Paper Airplane Champion."

"Well, congratulations. You're famous. I hope it was worth it."

"They'll never take me. My airplane fell apart."

Sofia banged a fist on the table. The salt and pepper shakers jumped.

"You got expelled! That's got to count for something."

"No, that's not a competitive category. Lots of kids get expelled."

Harvey placed a hand on Sofia's shoulder to calm her down.

"Danny, your mother and I are very disappointed in you."

Sofia erupted. "Disappointed? As in he forgot to take out the garbage? Really? **HE JUST RUINED HIS ENTIRE LIFE!**"

Paper Plane Champ

Paper Plane Chump

Danny, confined to his room, sat on the floor. His life was over and it was all because of the Ultimate Almanac and his stupid ideas.

He looked down at all his paper airplanes strewn across the floor. In a sudden fit of anger he swept them all together and crushed them into a giant ball so that none of them would ever fly again.

A key jiggled in the bedroom door. Danny quickly pushed the paper ball deep under his bed and out of sight. Harvey entered with a tray of food and placed it on the desk.

"I didn't do it to make trouble for you guys," Danny said.

"I know," Harvey said. "But as usual, you didn't think it through."

"I thought that if I got into the Ultimate Almanac, it would make me someone special."

"Doing well in school is a better way to be someone special."

"Does mom hate me?"

"She wants you to succeed."

"You mean get good grades."

"That's how the game is played."

"You know, for a game, it's not a lot of fun."

"You don't have a choice. None of us do."

Harvey left the room. Danny heard the door lock.

Harvey went to the kitchen and found Sofia eating Ben and Jerry's Chocolate Therapy straight from the quart container.

"Did he say anything?" she asked between bites.

"That he was sorry.   And that he was trying to prove himself." Harvey pulled a spoon from the drawer and went after the ice cream.

"Where does he get this from?" Sofia asked.

"Must be your side of the family."

Sofia shot Harvey a dirty look and pulled back, protecting the ice cream.

"He's not scared of us," she said. "That's the problem. When I was his age, I never did anything wrong because I knew my father would kill me."

Harvey pointed his spoon at the ice cream. "Are you going to share that with me?"

"No. I need it a lot more than you do right now."

"What if I admit that he gets it from my side of the family?"

Sofia softened and held out the container of ice cream. "That'll get you one spoonful."

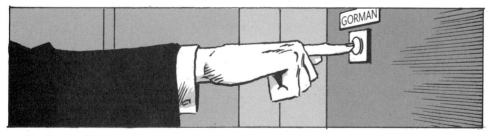

Sofia and Harvey were sitting at the table sharing the last of the ice cream when the doorbell rang.

Harvey looked at Sofia. "Expecting someone?" he asked. She shook her head.

"If it's that Congressional campaign that wants to plant a sign on our lawn," she said, "let me deal with them this time."

They put down their spoons and headed for the front door.

Harvey examined Doctor Ning's distorted figure through the lens of the peephole.

"He doesn't have a yard sign with him."

The bell chimed again. Harvey stepped back and opened the door. A gaunt, serious man in an impeccable black business suit with an American flag lapel pin stood before them. Further back, at the curb, they could see the shiny black limousine that had brought him.

"Doctor and Ms. Gorman?" Ning asked.

"Actually, I'm a doctor too," Sofia replied. "Sociology."

"That counts. Doctors Gorman, may I come in?"

"What's this about?" Harvey asked.

"The future," Ning replied grandly. "Danny's future."

Sofia suddenly recognized the man. "You're Doctor Ning. The Secretary of Education. You just got a medal." She turned to her husband, excited. "It's Doctor Ning, the Secretary of Education."

"Of the United States?" Harvey said. Sofia nodded enthusiastically. Ning breezed past them into the living room and stepped over to an ornate clock on the mantel.

"My goodness. Is that an 18th-century French ormolu?"

"I doubt it," Harvey said. "We picked it up at the Paris airport

with the last of our euros. It was either that clock or a model of the Eiffel Tower made out of dried spaghetti."

Sofia swooped in. "Can I offer you something, Mr. Secretary? Coffee, a glass of wine, chocolate milk?"

Ning smiled. "No thank you."

"So, this is about Danny?" Harvey asked.

"Yes."

"Not to question the inner workings of the government, but isn't it unusual for a member of the cabinet to get directly involved with a 7th grader?"

Ning looked squarely at the couple, offended. "Doctors Gorman, I'm responsible for all the children of this great country." Ning, Sofia, and Harvey settled around the coffee table in the living room. Ning turned to Harvey. "You're a dentist."

"That's right."

"How was your profession practiced 200 years ago?"

"Brutally, but they threw in a haircut."

Ning leaned in close. "Medicine, law, journalism and every other profession – except one – has been completely transformed in the last 200 years. Which one do you think is the exception?"

"Literary criticism?"

"Education. A 19th-century child transported to the present would be bewildered by everything he encountered...except a classroom, where he would still find a teacher lecturing to a row of desks."

Then...and...Now

Sofia, hoping to make a good impression, chimed in.

"That's very interesting. I never thought of it that way."

Ning continued. "I'm not surprised that Danny's struggling. He's a very smart boy, but the victim of an obsolete system."

"Danny's smart?" Harvey and Sofia said together.

"He performed exceptionally well on the Ypsilanti Multiphasic Inventory."

"The what?" Sofia asked.

"It was administered in kindergarten."

Harvey turned to his wife. "Must have been during one of those field trips."

Ning flicked open his leather briefcase and presented them with a thick booklet. "I can close the gap between his potential and his performance. *The Academy of Excellence and Transformation.* A model for the 21st century."

"Really?" Sofia asked.

"Why?" Harvey added.

"Right now Danny is a zero," Ning said. "When I turn him into a ten, it will be additional proof that my school works." Ning flipped to the contract at the end of the booklet. "All I need is your permission, which you give me by signing here."

Sofia searched her pockets. "Does anyone have a pen?"

"Where is this place?" Harvey asked.

"In Maine. It's a self-contained world of learning based on the latest research. Danny will live at the facility, protected from harmful influences...like the Ultimate Almanac."

"Does he get to come home?" Sofia asked. "Can we visit him?"

"Of course, but he has to earn that privilege. It's all in this booklet along with the latest student improvement studies."

Ning's cellphone chimed. He checked the message and abruptly stood. "There's a long waiting list. Most families would give anything to get their child in. But, of course, it's up to you."

Ning carefully placed an embossed, gold-tinged Secretary of Education business card on the table. "Consider your options. I'll hold his spot for 24 hours. I'll see myself out."

Harvey flipped through the Academy booklet, which was filled with impressive, glossy pictures.

"Consider your options," Sofia repeated, mimicking Ning's parting words. "Like we have any."

Harvey put down the booklet. "Danny's got to be part of the decision."

"Really? Going to school is his call now? Let's get him an even bigger computer and a McDonald's franchise while we're at it."

"That's not what—"

Sofia cut him off. "Ning's a certified genius. They gave him tenure at Harvard when he was twenty-three. What's your plan, dentist man? Home school?"

Harvey shrugged. "Exactly," Sofia said. "Now let's go up there together and start acting like parents."

THAT CRAZY KID! I'M CALLING 911!

WHAT GOOD IS THAT?

THEY WON'T DO ANYTHING FOR 24 HOURS!

YOU HAVE A BETTER IDEA?

YOU BET I DO!

YOUR ATTENTION PLEASE...

GRAUHUND BUS LINES

BUS

BUS 16, LOCAL SERVICE TO QUEETS, QUINAULT, AND QUILLAYUTE, NOW BOARDING AT GATE NUMBER FIVE.

Take the BUS

ARRIVALS →

SODA

A PATROL CAR SPOTTED DANNY AT THE BUS STATION. I'M GLAD YOU CALLED. IT WOULD HAVE BEEN MUCH MORE DIFFICULT TO FIND HIM ONCE HE LEFT TOWN.

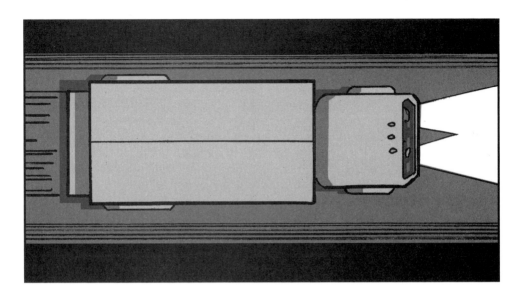

Chapter 3

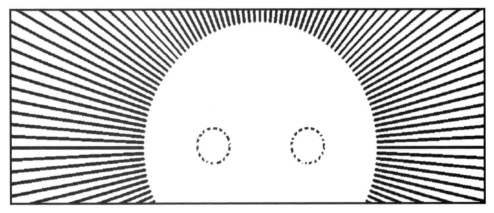

Danny ran his fingers along the padded walls, desperate to find a way out. Getting kidnapped was bad enough. Being forced to listen to Stuart Green was even worse.

The annoying child actor continued: "Hundreds of really smart people from the best companies in the world have designed this place to be fun and teach you everything you need to know to have a good life. The Academy of Excellence and Transformation is based on..."

The **3 CORE PRINCIPLES**

1.

LEARN to EARN!

That means rewards when you get something right. Grown-ups get paid. So should you!

2.

LEARN, don't CHURN!

We know what's important and we're not going to let you waste time on stuff that doesn't matter!

3.

YOU ARE your GRADE!

You're a student.
That's your job.
Own it!

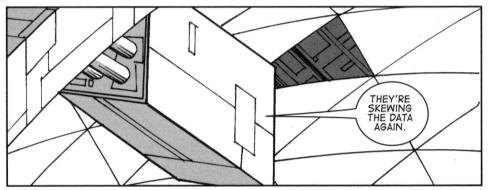

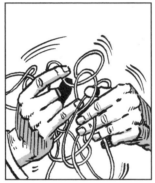

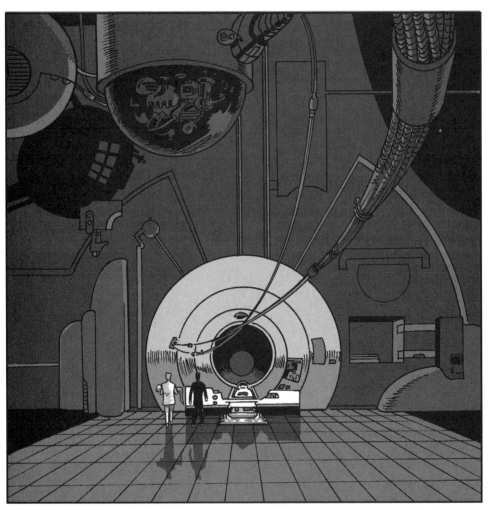

Danny lay curled up into a ball, hands pressed firmly against his ears in a futile attempt to block out Stuart Green, who hadn't shut up since first appearing at the beginning of the trip and was now giving Danny a history lesson. "In April 1775, Revere made his famous midnight ride to Lexington and Concord to warn the Patriots of the British advance."

The van came to a stop. Danny jumped to his feet and banged on the walls, shouting to be heard over Stuart Green.

"Hello! Anybody there?! I've been kidnapped!"

Stuart Green got louder, drowning him out.

"Revere was captured by the British in Lexington before he could reach Concord."

"Call the police!"

No answer. Danny slumped against the wall, defeated.

The van stopped moving. Stuart Green bleeped off the screen mid-sentence and was replaced by a whooping siren, accompanied by flashing red lights. The van rocked back and forth, like it was being hoisted into the air. What on earth was going on?

 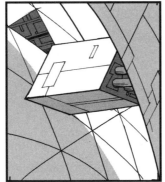 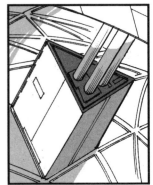

The entire compartment tipped on its side and opened. Danny tumbled out onto the floor of a new room. The breach in the wall that had let him in quickly slid back into place.

Danny stood up, caught his breath, and looked around.

The space was small, modern, and clean. A blue jumpsuit with the Department of Education insignia on the pocket lay neatly on the bed. Several colorful magazines with titles like "Grammar

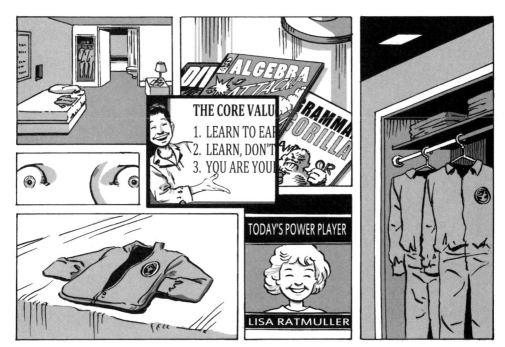

Gorilla" and "Algebra Attack!" were spread across the night table.

Prominently displayed on the wall was a framed inspirational poster with the school's three core principles: "LEARN TO EARN. LEARN, DON'T CHURN. YOU ARE YOUR GRADE." And right under that, a video screen featuring today's "Power Player," grinning 14-year-old Lisa Ratmuller.

Danny entered the tiny bathroom and found soap molded into the Department of Education insignia, towels, and an electric toothbrush.

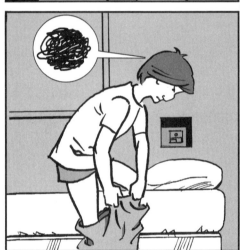

Danny stepped out of his room and found himself gazing down at what looked like a vast shopping mall filled with kids.

He followed the balcony until he reached an elevator. The shiny metal doors swished open and two boys, roughly his age, burst out. He tried to stop them, but they ran away, laughing and chasing one another.

Danny entered the elevator and pressed "G." Nothing happened, so he pressed the button again. Suddenly the white walls came alive and "one squared" written mathematically next to an equal sign appeared. A friendly female voice addressed him from the ceiling: "Please use the marker provided."

Danny looked around, spotted a marker in the corner, and wrote "1" after the equal sign. Cheering erupted from the loudspeaker, animated confetti fell down the walls, and the elevator whisked him down to the ground floor.

The elevator doors opened and Danny entered the mall.

HIKE
Just Learn It.

A looping roller coaster dominated the center of the giant space. Kids everywhere strolled in and out of the fast food franchises and corporate-sponsored gaming arcades with names like Chemistry Combat, Newton's Nut House, and Grammar Sledgehammer.

Some kids wore jumpsuits, like his, while others were dressed in trendy clothes with only an Academy of Excellence and Transformation badge pinned to their shirts.

Grownups in bright yellow outfits circulated, keeping an eye on everything. One of them glanced down at his handheld computer and made a beeline for Danny, hand thrust out.

Danny eyed him warily. "Do I know you?" he asked.

Ken pointed at the Department of Education seal on Danny's jumpsuit. "Not yet, but I know you. The chip on your badge transmits all your personal data to me in real time. At The Academy for Excellence and Transformation every student is an individual with unique learning needs."

"What are you? A teacher?"

"A facilitator," Ken replied. "We don't have teachers. Or classrooms. Or set lessons." Ken was like a creepy uncle hellbent on proving that he can relate to kids. "My job is to help you create your own learning adventure," he continued. "Take you to the water, so to speak, so that you may drink."

"How about you take me to the exit so that I may leave?" Danny snapped back. "I was kidnapped."

"On your parents' instructions. Technically, that's busing."

This was going nowhere fast. Danny bolted, running down the walkway, searching for a way out. Ken followed briskly, without breaking into a run.

Danny ducked into a cave-like arcade called Chemistry Combat. As his eyes adjusted to the dark he found himself surrounded by boys and girls playing first-person shooter games against an army of molecules.

"Hey! How do you get out of this place?" Danny yelled. Some of the kids looked up, annoyed at being distracted from their games. Danny spotted Ken methodically coming toward him like The Terminator, and ran.

Danny opened his eyes. The last thing he remembered was some dude with a crew cut grabbing his neck. The man sitting beside him came slowly into focus. It was Doctor Ning, the source of all his problems.

"I'm sorry, Danny. You were going to hurt someone, or yourself. I can't let that happen." Ning held out a cup of something, probably poison. "Drink this." Danny pushed the cup away. "It's just water. I'm Doctor Ning. This is my school."

"I know who you are. You can't keep me here."

Ning smiled and leaned in closer. "Danny, my friend, the only way out is through the center."

"What the hell does that mean?"

"It means that your parents placed you in my hands. This is your journey now. There is nothing else. For a smart kid like you The Academy of Excellence and Transformation could be paradise. I'll make a prediction: when it is finally time for you to leave, you'll want to stay."

"I'll take that water now."

Ning handed him the glass. Danny tipped it over and slowly poured the contents on the couch, staring at Ning for a reaction. Ning didn't flinch.

"There's somebody I want you to meet."

Ning snapped his fingers, the door opened, and a self-assured fourteen-year-old girl with a page-boy haircut entered the room.

Chapter 4

Danny and Codie entered the cafeteria, a who's who of the hottest fast food franchises in the world.

Codie grabbed an apple. Danny eyed the mouth-watering choices and finally pulled a triple bacon cheeseburger with special sauce from the shelf.

"There's a free table over there," he said.

"You have to pay for that first."

"With what? I don't have any money."

"With Smart Bucks from the games."

Codie handed the cashier her Smart Bucks credit card. "I got him."

"So, if I don't learn and earn I—"

"Starve."

"Seriously?"

"Why do you think kids go to school in the first place? Guess what happens to grown-ups who can't do anything useful?"

"This is totally screwed up."

"It's important to understand money and responsibility. Make an effort, is all. I doubt they'll let you actually starve. I mean, like, completely to death."

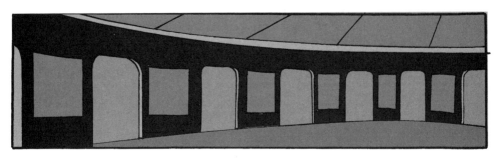

Chapter 5

After hours spent clawing and twisting around in bed like a cat rolled up in a bath towel, Danny finally drifted off to sleep. Twelve minutes later he was jolted awake by the room lights flashing on and off in time to brainlessly optimistic music that was suddenly blaring from the audio speakers.

He tried to bury himself beneath the covers, but it was no use. He poked his head out. The clock on the wall read 6:00 AM, next to a video portrait of the Academy of Excellence and Transformation Featured Power Player of the Day: Dorit.

Danny rolled out of bed, slipped into his jumpsuit, and headed for the door. As he turned the handle the pleasant female voice chimed: "Please make your bed."

Hell no. Danny twisted the handle. Locked.

"Please make your bed."

He tried again. And again.

"Please make your bed. Please make your bed."

"What are you, my mother?"

The voice didn't answer. Resigned, Danny made the damn bed and tried the handle again.

"Please brush your teeth."

"Seriously?"

"Please brush your teeth."

Danny kicked the door.

"Violence is not the answer."

"Depends on the question."

He headed for the bathroom and brushed his teeth with the talking toothbrush.

"Seven times seven is forty-nine. Eight times seven is…"

Teeth clean, he tried the door again. It opened.

"Have nice day. Make good choices."

Chapter 6

In the dim confines of the Solitary cell, time—and Stuart Green—dragged on...

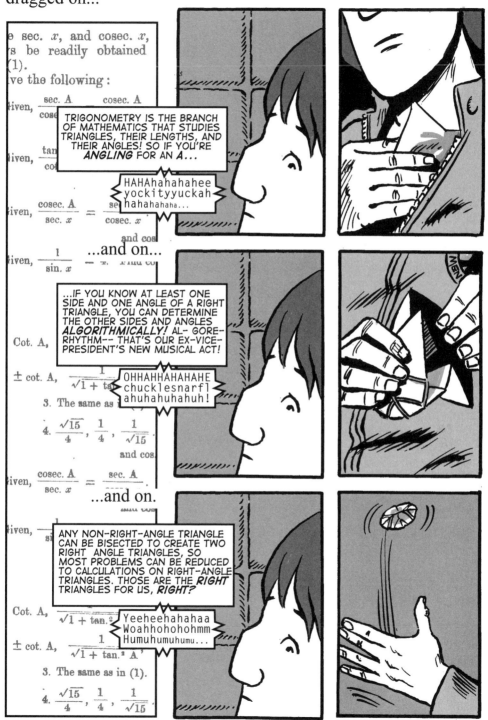

...and on...

...and on.

Danny examined his tiny winged creation with awe. He had solved the gravity activation enigma, a problem that had confounded paper airplane designers since the Egyptians started using papyrus reeds in 3500 BC.

The Trigonometry clown abruptly stopped mid sentence. Danny looked up. The screen was blank. The cell door opened, Kaczor stood in the entrance.

"On your feet."

Danny stepped out into the Mall. Nothing had changed.

"Now go learn something."

Kaczor shoved him along and turned away. Danny wandered aimlessly for a spell and then spotted Codie at the chessboards.

Codie began speaking quickly, just loud enough to be heard over the clatter of the roller coaster.

"This ride lasts exactly 143 seconds. They can't pick up our voices because of the screams. There are cameras everywhere, even in the dorms."

"Also, the food has meds. Are you ADHD, bipolar, hyperactive, depressed, anxious, violent, Oedipal, Asperger's, anorexic?"

"I think I have attention issues."

"Whatever. Stick with fresh fruit, vegetables, and sealed recognizable brands, if you can."

"I thought you'd escaped."

"Garbage chute's a dead end."

"Was that your first try?"

"Fourth. If you're an outlier, if you can't adapt to the system and get bad grades that pull down the averages, they do something to you. Your grades go up but you're not the same. Scream."

"What?"

"Scream. So they won't get suspicious."

"Do you remember Eric Goodpaster, the Ultimate Almanac Mimicry champion?" Codie asked. "He's the greatest! He's amazing. Not as amazing as you, of course."

"Come with me," Codie said.

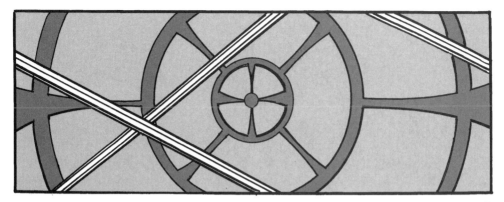

"THE ONLY WAY OUT IS THROUGH THE CENTER."

WOW!

OH, HI, DANNY.

THE ONLY WAY OUT...

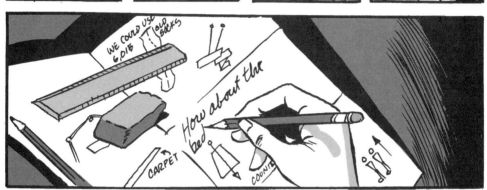

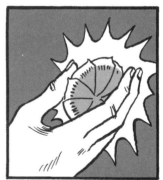

THANKS FOR THOSE COMIC BOOKS. I MISS YOU GUYS.

I'M STARTING TO LIKE IT HERE.

IT'S LIKE REGULAR SCHOOL, BUT THEY MAKE IT MORE INTERESTING AND GIVE ME TIME TO LEARN AT MY OWN SPEED.

LOOK HER
PRESS REC

THE TEACHERS ARE GREAT. ACTUALLY WE CALL THEM FACILITATORS. IT HAS SOMETHING TO DO WITH WATER.

REC STOP

I FEEL REALLY BAD ABOUT ALL THE TIMES I EMBARRASSED YOU BY GETTING INTO TROUBLE.

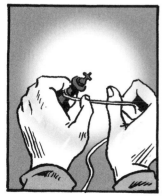

PTOO!

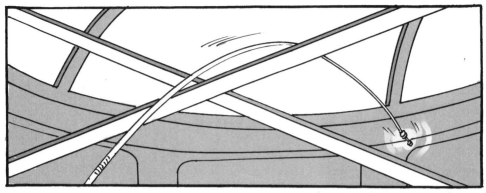

WHAT'S THAT KID UP TO?

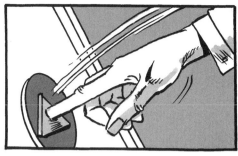

Chapter 8

I SEE THEM!

THIS IS FOX ONE! THE CHICKENS ARE CORNERED. FOLLOW MY SIGNAL!

I READ YOU LOUD AND CLEAR, FOX ONE! ON MY WAY!

TWO OF YOU CIRCLE AROUND TO THE RIGHT! MOVE IT!

Ning pulled at the string puppy. His life's work, his reputation, gone. Sunk beneath the waves just like those worthless kids.

Spitting?! Paper airplanes?! As a kid he had briefly flirted with pointless skills like that. Fortunately his mother put a stop to it and set him straight. He had worked his way up to Secretary of Education by not wasting time and by focusing exclusively on things that mattered…but now that could all disappear.

The puppy suddenly broke apart in his hands and unraveled. Ning groaned.

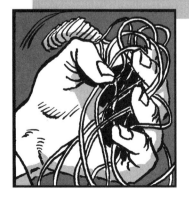

There was no way he would ever be able to knot it back together. That puppy had kept him company since he was a boy. And now it was just a long piece of string.

"Sir?"

Ning looked up and found Kaczor standing at attention.

"What do you want?"

"I accept full responsibility for what happened and tender my resignation."

Ning pulled at the string. "When your services are no longer required, I'll fire you."

"But it was my fault, sir."

"Which makes it my fault." Ning threw the useless clump of string against the wall. "Unless…" Ning fell silent, deep in thought, until finally Kaczor couldn't take it anymore.

"Unless what, sir?"

"Unless it's the Almanac's fault."

"The Farmers' Almanac?"

"Think about it. Danny's obsession with the Almanac got him expelled from school. Codie was an Almanac Champion. It follows, then, that those kids attempted a dangerous stunt because the Almanac told them to do it. Correct?"

Before Kaczor could answer Ning jumped to his feet and jabbed his index finger into Kaczor's chest.

"It's not our fault. The Ultimate Almanac needs to be shut down and the people behind it arrested!"

Chapter 9

ARE THEY...?

SOAKED, BUT THEY'LL BE FINE.

THE ULTIMATE ALMANAC?

IT'S A CULT THAT COERCES CHILDREN INTO DOING DANGEROUS STUNTS.

DANNY AND CODIE THOUGHT THEY COULD FLY WITH THE HELP OF A FEW PAPER AIRPLANES.

GREAT SCOTT!

MR. PRESIDENT, EVERYTHING WE'VE WORKED FOR IS AT RISK. YOU MUST COME OUT AGAINST THE ALMANAC!

SHUT IT DOWN!

ARREST THE PEOPLE RESPON-SIBLE!

BUT HOW...

IF YOU DON'T ACT THEY'LL BLAME YOU AND THE ACADEMY OF EXCELLENCE AND TRANSFORMATION!

WHAT ABOUT THE PARENTS?

LEGALLY, WE'RE PROTECTED. THEY SIGNED A BULLETPROOF CONTRACT.

BUT MORE TO THE POINT, I'M CERTAIN THAT UNDER YOUR LEADERSHIP, SIR...

...THEY'LL PUT THEIR GRIEF TO WORK CONSTRUCTIVELY, TO SAVE OTHER CHILDREN.

LIKE *MOTHERS AGAINST TEXTING?*

PRECISELY.

SHORE OBSERVERS SAY BOATS HAVE BEEN SCOURING THE OCEAN NEAR THE ACADEMY FOR SEVERAL HOURS.

MYSTERY SEARCH CONTINUES

WHAT THEY'RE SEARCHING FOR, NO ONE KNOWS.

THE DEPARTMENT OF EDUCATION HAS DECLINED TO COMMENT.

NEWS AT ELEVEN

DING DONG DING DONG

I'LL DEAL WITH IT.

IT'S DOCTOR NING! WHAT'S GOING ON?

IS HE IN TROUBLE? WHAT DID HE DO?

I'M SORRY TO DISTURB YOU AT THIS HOUR...

...I'M AFRAID I HAVE UNPLEASANT NEWS.

OH, NO! SOMETHING'S HAPPENED TO DANNY!

Danny blinked awake, surprised to be alive. The first thing that came into focus was the elderly couple at the foot of his bed. He turned and saw Codie, still unconscious, on the bed next to him.

"She'll wake up soon," the old lady assured him.

Danny appraised the strange couple. "Is this a hospital?"

"You could call it a submarine tender," the old man answered.

"An infirmary," the old lady corrected. "Don't confuse him, dear."

Danny noticed something on the table near the bed that looked like a cross between a scalpel and a thermometer. He had no idea who these creepy people were and he didn't plan on sticking around to find out. Extending his arms like he was stretching after a long sleep, he suddenly shifted his weight and lunged for the strange instrument.

"Careful! That's very delicate!" the old man shouted. Danny ignored him, wielding the instrument like a knife.

"Whatever this is, I'm not afraid to use it. Nobody has to get hurt, but I'm leaving with the girl. Wake her up."

The old man reached into his pocket and lobbed a tangle of string at Danny, holding onto one end. Somehow it wrapped itself into an elaborate knot around the instrument and, presto, Danny's hand was empty and the instrument was back on the bench.

Danny looked up, incredulous. "How'd you do that?"

Before the old man could answer, Codie leaped from her bed holding the sheet out like a net and landed on the couple, trapping them underneath.

Danny and Codie dashed from the room and down a long corridor lined with closed bulkhead doors until they saw sunlight streaming down a spiral staircase up ahead. A way out! They clambered up the stairs and found themselves on the deck of a yacht, in the middle of the ocean, with nowhere else to go.

Suddenly a voice materialized out of thin air right in front of them: "Stop. We mean you no harm."

Danny looked at Codie. "Did you hear that?"

Codie nodded. "Freaky."

The old couple, out of breath, slowly emerged on deck at the top of the stairs. Danny and Codie backed away.

"We mean you no harm," the same voice repeated, this time coming from the old lady.

"How'd you do that?" Codie asked.

"Throw my voice? It takes a lifetime of practice. Like spitting."

"What do you want with us?" Danny demanded. "Who are you?"

The old man smiled and pantomimed tipping his hat. "Mr. Prime, at your service."

"And Ms. Prime," said the old lady, curtseying.

The display of manners did nothing to relieve Codie's suspicions. "What is all this? Who do you work for?"

"The Prime," the old couple answered together.

"You just said your name was Prime," Danny snapped.

"Actually, that's an honorary title, like Mr. President."

"Or Ms. Prime Minister," Ms. Prime added. Mr. Prime smiled at the modest pun.

"What's your real name then?" Danny asked.

"That is not your concern at the moment," Ms. Prime said. "It is very important that we tell you only what you need to know."

"Why?"

Ms. Prime's eyes narrowed. "Because anything more might affect your development."

"Our organization began six hundred years ago in Italy, before the Renaissance," Mr. Prime said. "We help outliers, children that don't fit in. Like you two. And your friends, the other Ultimate Almanac champions. We're the ones who started the Almanac as a way to find candidates."

"Candidates? For what?" Codie shot back.

"The Prime, of course," Mr. Prime replied.

Danny had heard enough. "You're both crazy."

Mr. Prime stepped closer. "Please hear us out. Then you may do as you wish."

LET ME TELL YOU ABOUT OUR ORGANIZATION. AS I SAID, IT BEGAN SIX HUNDRED YEARS AGO, IN PRE-RENAISSANCE ITALY.

THE STORY OF THE PRIME

Every generation gives birth to a handful of kids that become obsessed with useless activities that never appear on tests. If it weren't for The Prime, those kids would be written off and cast aside.

Which is a shame because they're the most important people in the world. Their gift is the unknown. They're the ones who create new paths where none existed before.

Our founders began by supporting a small group of children that sparked the Renaissance.

Like Leonardo da Vinci. He was the illegitimate son of a peasant woman.

The Prime set him up in Verrocchio's workshop.

RELOCATION REPORT

ROXIE DORFF
ULTIMATE ALMANAC PROJECTILE CHAMPION

STATUS: In custody.

...hours Teams 16 and 30 ...d subject's home. Parents ...ubject had left for a ...ld. Team 16 followed ...30 circled around back.

> I'M OPTIMISTIC THAT WE CAN UNDO THE ALMANAC'S DAMAGE.

We spotted subject working on a large wooden device which seemed to be a sort of catapult. Subject ignored our order to halt and climbed onto device.

Before we could apprehend her, subject sat in catapult bucket.

Catapult launched subject over heads of Team. Subject landed approximately 500 feet away.

However Team 16 was able to encircle subject and took subject into custody through use of non-lethal persuasion.

RELOCATION REPORT

JAVIER SABENORIO
ULTIMATE ALMANAC OBSOLETE TECHNOLOGY CHAMPION

STATUS: In custody.

...000 hours Team 24 approached ...in disused barn. Subject ...r knock, so Team forced ...entry.

THE CHILDREN ARE BEING TAKEN TO OUR MODEL SCHOOL IN MAINE...

Some sort of early warning system warned subject of our approach. Subject fled into warehouse.

Team pursued subject. Two Team members were struck by a trap resembling an old "disco ball."

Subject evaded capture by using a variety of strange devices.

DING!

Subject misdirected Team using an antique "gramophone."

HE'S OVER THERE BEHIND THAT TANK!

It became necessary to deploy tear gas to subdue subject.

After subject was pacified, tasers were employed to ensure continued compliance.

RELOCATION REPORT

KIM PARTON
ULTIMATE ALMANAC ILLUSION CHAMPION

STATUS: In custody.

Team 7 gained entry into subject's home using ram vehicle. Subject was ~~in~~-home art studio. Subject ~~d~~ order to surrender.

...THE ACADEMY OF EXCELLENCE AND TRANSFORMATION!

Subject appeared to be drawing on floor of studio.

Suddenly a large sink hole opened in floor. Team barely avoided falling into hole.

Team worked its way around perimeter of sink hole toward subject. Subject started to run toward sink hole. Hole proved to be...

...a clever drawing. Subject tried to escape, but...

...team overtook her and applied appropriate force.

Once subject was restrained, Team leader attempted to notify remainder of team of situation.

BRING UP THE VAN, BOYS, WE'VE...

AWWRK!!

BONK!

Danny and Codie exchanged a wary glance. Maybe the Primes weren't crazy, just demented. Something like that had happened to Danny's grandparents, but they hadn't had a submarine full of fancy gadgets at their disposal.

"Why didn't you talk to Ning's mom?" Danny asked.

"We did. It's against the rules, but we did," Ms. Prime answered. "It didn't help. We lost him anyway." Ms. Prime looked down. The consequences of their failure still hurt.

Mr. Prime continued. "His mother told him about us before she died. He was furious and has used all his power in the government to track us down. He wanted to know why he had been excluded from The Prime and if he could still join."

"Did he ever find you?" Codie asked.

"No," Mr. Prime answered. "And even if he had, there's absolutely nothing we could have done for him. It was too late. You can't get your childhood back. The tragedy is that his anger with us inspired him to create The Academy of Excellence and Transformation. If his mother had forced him to conform and give up his peculiar passions, he was going to make sure that every child in the country suffered the same fate."

Danny and Codie stared at the bizarre device. It looked like something you'd find in a hospital basement or Doctor Frankenstein's garage.

Mr. Prime continued. "It resets the brain, like updating the operating system on a malfunctioning computer. The quirks disappear. Grades improve."

"Which, sadly, encourages the practice," Ms. Prime added. "It's hard enough on an average child, but the effect on a Prime candidate is devastating. Just one session can destroy the wiring that makes each of us unique."

"You're the ones with the submarine," Codie blurted. "Blow the place up or something!"

"It doesn't work that way,." Mr. Prime answered. "We don't confront the establishment directly. We wouldn't stand a chance. We influence the course of history through children, and right now you two are our best and, I'm afraid to say, our only hope. *We need your help.*"

RELOCATION REPORT

OLIVER KRIMP
ULTIMATE ALMANAC CAMOUFLAGE CHAMPION

STATUS: In transit.

Subject has been remanded to DOE custody and is presently en route to Academy of Excellence and Transformation.

Chapter 10

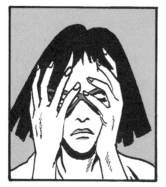

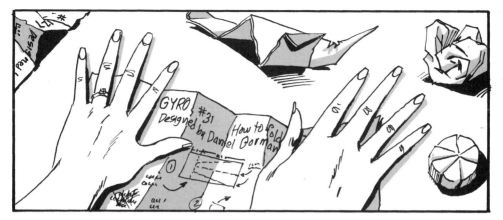

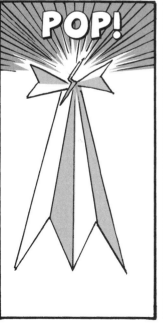  

HOLEY SHIRT! IT'S *DANNY GORMAN!*

NUMBER SIX! THE GORMAN KID IS RIGHT BEHIND YOU! *BRING HIM IN!*

ROGER! I SEE HIM.

Harvey nursed a mug of tea that had gone cold an hour ago and stared out the kitchen window at the maple tree in front of the house. Danny used to be fascinated by that tree and the seed-pods that spun elegantly from its branches in the spring.

Sofia joined him. She was carrying a handful of folded paper and wearing a familiar expression that told him she had already made a decision for both of them but was going to ask for his opinion anyway.

"What's up?" he asked.

Instead of answering, Sofia tossed one of the folded papers into the air. It was an airplane, and sailed elegantly in a closing spiral, turning lazily on its horizontal axis, until it came to rest on the floor like a rocket ship, nose pointing straight up.

Harvey was impressed. "Where—"

"Danny's room."

Sofia threw a handful of small polygon discs at him, like confetti. One by one, they popped open into airplanes and coasted gently to the ground.

"He's different," she said.. "I'll give you that. But not suicidal. And he's not an idiot. If he jumped, he had it figured out. They're not telling us the truth."

Harvey stared at his wife, fearful, frightened and ecstatic at the same time. "You think he's alive?"

"If he's not, then where's the body?" she shot back.

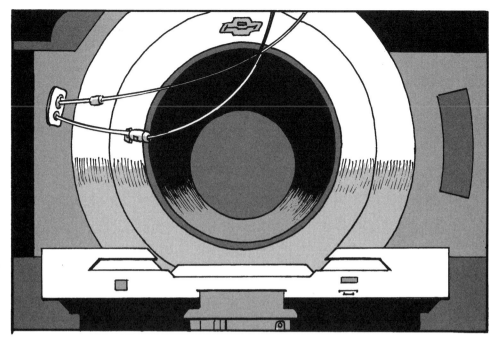

Chapter 11

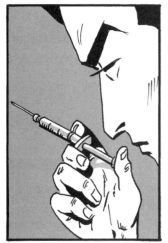

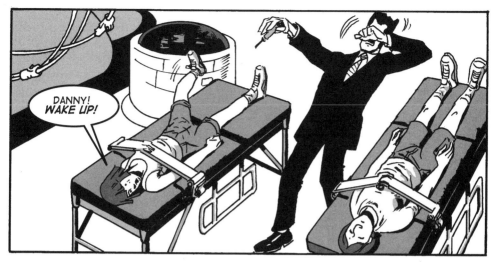

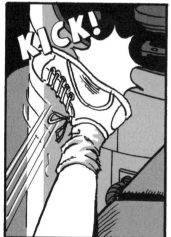

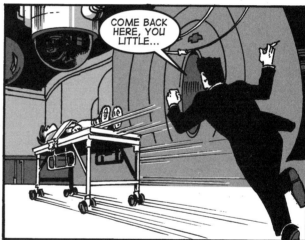

WHACK!

SO THEY CAUGHT YOU, TOO?

I'M NOT *THAT* LAME!

I SAW YOU GO DOWN AND RAN OVER TO HELP.

REALLY?

DON'T TAKE IT PERSONALLY.

HERE'S NING'S ACCESS CARD! IT MAY BE OUR TICKET OUT OF HERE.

Chapter 12

The reporters and camera crews packed up their gear. Now that the last Ultimate Almanac kid was inside the school, it was time to go home.

Suddenly a Chevy Malibu fishtailed around the corner and screeched dramatically to a stop in cloud of dust. Harvey, at the wheel, grinned. The last time he'd pulled a stunt like this was with his dad's Dodge Dart Swinger in high school.

"Open the gate!" Sofia yelled at the booth beside the ferry gate.

A guard poked his head from the booth's window like a turtle from its shell. "Who are you?" he asked.

"We're here to find out what happened to our son, Danny. So let us in. Now! "

The guard's head disappeared back inside.

The Press, curious, stopped their packing and surrounded the car. A short man with a handlebar mustache and a pencil behind one ear stepped forward. "Mr. and Ms. Gorman, are you questioning the government's account of what happened to Danny?" he asked.

"That's exactly what we're doing," Sofia answered.

The reporter reached for his pencil. "On what evidence?"

Sofia's eyes narrowed. She dug into her pocket, pulled out a handful of the folded polygon discs, and flung them out the window. Just as they had in the Gormans' kitchen, the discs rose into the air and popped open into tiny paper airplanes. The press gasped and chased after the little airplanes like they were $100 bills.

Harvey turned to Sofia. "Did we take out the extra insurance on the rental?"

"I think so."

Harvey revved the engine, foot on the brake. The car's exhaust billowed. The guard's turtle-head popped out of the booth again. Harvey dropped his foot from the brake. The wheels sprayed gravel onto the Press and sent the car flying forward into the gate, snapping the barrier arm like a Popsicle stick.

The airbags exploded. Harvey and Sofia swatted them away, ditched the car, and headed for the ferry. The Press poured in after them like milk from a knocked-over glass.

The ferry captain stood bravely at the dock, guarding his ship. "This is a restricted—"

Sofia shoved him into the water and boarded the ferry, followed by her husband and a crowd of reporters suddenly anxious to cover the story.

Chapter 13

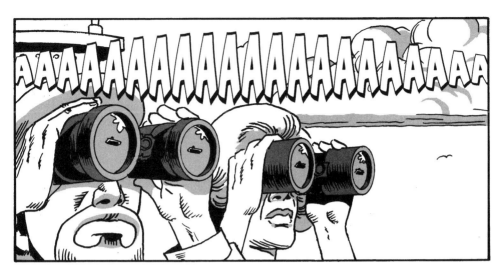

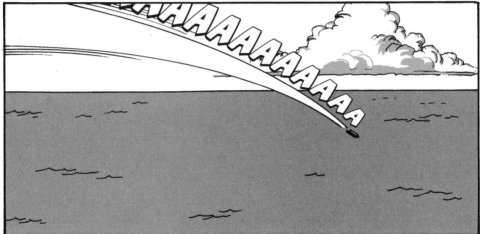

About the Creators

DAVID ULLENDORFF

is an award-winning filmmaker and writer whose work has been featured on TNT, A&E, and Showtime. He is also president and co-founder of Mathnasium, a company dedicated to teaching math to kids with over 1,000 Learning Centers worldwide.

RON HARRIS

began his career illustrating newspaper comic strips. He later worked as an artist and writer at Marvel and DC Comics. During the 90's he was a designer and storyboard artist for TV cartoons like *Carmen Sandiego* and *Ghostbusters*. In recent years Ron has drawn storyboards for feature films.